Meet the Beaver

Suzanne Buckingham

PowerKiDS press
New York

Published in 2009 by The Rosen Publishing Group, Inc.
29 East 21st Street, New York, NY 10010

First Edition

Editor: Joanne Randolph
Book Design: Greg Tucker
Photo Researcher: Jessica Gerweck

Photo Credits: Back cover, cover (logo), cover photo, pp. 5, 9, 10, 20 Shutterstock.com; p. 6 © JUNIORS BILDARCHIV; pp. 12–13 © Superstock, Inc./Superstock; p. 15 © Kevin Moloney/Getty Images; p. 16 © Lynda Richardson/Peter Arnold Inc.; p. 19 © Aurora/Getty Images.

Library of Congress Cataloging-in-Publication Data

Buckingham, Suzanne.
  Meet the beaver / Suzanne Buckingham. — 1st ed.
      p. cm. — (Scales and tails)
  ISBN 978-1-4042-4502-0 (library binding)
  1. Beavers—Juvenile literature. I. Title.
  QL737.R632B83 2009
  599.37—dc22
                                      2008007741

Manufactured in the United States of America

Contents

Busy Beavers

Beavers are hardworking animals. They like to chop down trees and build with wood. Beavers are always busy searching for food, too. They like to eat leaves, grass, branches, and **bark** from certain trees.

These furry **mammals** are great swimmers. Their **webbed** back feet are powerful paddles in the water. Beavers also have long, flat tails, which help them swim fast. Although beavers live in places where it gets cold, they keep busy in the winter, too. Their thick fur helps keep them warm in icy waters.

Beavers are rodents, as are rats and mice. A beaver's teeth never stop growing, so it must chew hard things, like wood, to keep its teeth short.

This beaver is carrying wood to help build its home. Beavers spend much of their time in the water.

Two Kinds of Beavers

There are only two different kinds of beavers. The American beaver is found all over the United States and Mexico, except for deserts. It also lives in southern and central Canada. Eurasian beavers live in the northern part of Europe and Asia. Both the American and Eurasian beavers make their homes in forests near freshwater lakes, ponds, and rivers.

These two kinds of beavers are alike in many ways, but they also have several differences. For example, American beavers have wider tails and larger heads than Eurasian beavers. American beavers usually have larger litters, or groups of babies, too.

A Cozy Coat

A beaver has a beautiful brown coat made of two kinds of fur. The soft fur next to its skin is called underfur. Underfur holds in a beaver's body heat.

The outer coat is made of long, thick fur. A beaver has **oil glands** under its tail. It rubs the oil produced by these glands on its outside coat to make it **waterproof**.

When the weather becomes cold in the fall, a beaver's coat grows in thicker. This new fur helps it stay warm during winter. In the spring a beaver sheds, or loses, its extra winter fur.

The beaver's thick fur coat keeps the beaver warm while it swims in the water. The outer coat keeps the beaver's body nice and dry.

Here you can see a beaver lodge. It has been in this pond so long that grass has grown on the top.

The Beaver Lodge

Beavers make wood homes, called lodges, in lakes, ponds, and rivers. They build their lodges in slow-moving water that is more than 4 feet (1 m) deep. To gather the wood they need for building, beavers chew through small trees with their sharp teeth. Then they cut the fallen trees into pieces.

Beavers place pieces of wood under the water to start a new lodge. They use rocks to hold the wood down. Beavers keep adding logs, mud, and rocks to the pile until the lodge is finished. A beaver family, called a colony, lives together in one lodge.

The Beaver

With their strong paddle-shaped tails and webbed back feet, beavers can swim at a speed of up to 2 miles per hour (3 km/h).

A beaver's tail can be from about 10 to 20 inches (25-50 cm) long.

Tail Tales

- Beavers have lived on Earth for about 35 **million** years.
- Adult beavers eat 1 ½ to 2 pounds (.7–.9 kg) of food every day.
- Beavers weigh around 45 to 60 pounds (20–27 kg).
- Beavers are nocturnal, which means they are usually awake at night and sleeping during the day.
- Beavers use their four front teeth called incisors to cut wood. A beaver can cut through a 6-inch- (15 cm) thick tree with its sharp orange teeth in less than 20 minutes!
- Beavers usually stay underwater for about 3 to 5 minutes. Some can stay under for as long as 15 minutes.
- A beaver uses its nose to tell it if enemies are near. A beaver's sharp sense of smell is about 100 times better than a human's.
- Beavers can live to be 20 years old.

A Beaver's Tail

The beaver is well known for its tail, which is covered with large, black **scales**. Although this tail is flat, it is very heavy. Some of a beaver's extra fat is stored there.

A beaver needs its tail to do many things. When a beaver stands on its two back legs to chew trees, it places its tail on the ground to keep its body upright. This oval-shaped tail also acts like a paddle. A beaver uses it to swim faster and make turns in the water. By slapping its tail on top of the water, a beaver lets other beavers know danger is near.

This is a close-up look at a beaver's tail. A beaver needs its tail to swim, to cut down trees, and to keep itself safe.

Here a mother beaver swims with her two kits. The kits will stay with their mother until they are two years old.

Through the Years

Mother beavers have their litters in the spring. There can be up to four baby beavers in a litter. Baby beavers are called kits. When a kit is one year old, it is called a yearling.

A beaver becomes a juvenile when it is two years old. A juvenile is old enough to move out of the family lodge and take care of itself. The following winter, a juvenile turns into an adult. An adult beaver searches for a **mate** to stay with the rest of its life. Soon, this beaver pair will have new kits of their own.

Baby Beavers

Baby beavers are about 15 inches (38 cm) long when they are born. Kits usually weigh a little less than 1 pound (.5 kg) at birth. Newborns have brown, red, or black fur. Their eyes are open, and they can swim within 24 hours of birth. Kits drink milk from their mothers right away. When babies are three days old, they begin eating soft plants.

Most kits are ready to leave the family lodge for long periods of time when they are a month old. These kits like to swim around and search for food.

This kit has gone out on its own to find food. It will head back to the lodge when it is done.

Beaver dams cause problems when they flood land on which people or animals live. Here the beaver dam is the long wall of sticks in front of the lodge.

Nature's Helper

Busy beavers not only build lodges, they also make dams. A dam is a pile of branches and logs that slows down moving water in rivers and streams. A beaver dam does not allow much water through, so water often backs up and forms a pond. These ponds make new homes for water animals and supply drinking water for land animals.

Over time, some ponds turn into **wetlands**. Animals need new wetland areas because people have destroyed many of Earth's wetlands. Wetlands help clean nature because they get rid of **pollutants** in water.

Saving the Beaver

People have trapped beavers for hundreds of years. Many people like to use beavers' beautiful coats to make hats and clothing. In the 1500s, French **explorers** began trading with Native North Americans for beaver furs. Later, the Dutch and English sent ships to America for beaver furs. By the early 1700s, beavers were nearly **extinct** in parts of North America.

In the late 1800s, people realized they needed to save beavers. New laws were written to **protect** beavers from hunters. Large wooded parks were made where beavers could live safely. Today, nature groups are still working hard to protect beavers.

Glossary

bark (BARK) The hard outside covering on trees.

explorers (ek-SPLOR-erz) People who travel over little-known lands.

extinct (ek-STINKT) None remaining.

mammals (MA-mulz) Warm-blooded animals that have a backbone and hair, breathe air, and feed milk to their young.

mate (MAYT) A partner for making babies.

million (MIL-yun) A very large number, or a thousand thousands.

oil glands (OY-ul GLANDZ) Parts of the body that produce oil.

pollutants (puh-LOO-tants) Humanmade waste that harms Earth's air, land, or water.

protect (pruh-TEKT) To keep safe.

scales (SKAYLZ) The thin, dry pieces of skin that form the outer covering of some animals, such as snakes.

waterproof (WAH-ter-proof) Cannot get wet.

webbed (WEBD) Having skin between the toes, as do ducks, frogs, and other animals that swim.

wetlands (WET-landz) Land with a lot of water in the soil.

Index

A
American beaver, 7
Asia, 7

C
Canada, 7
coat(s), 8, 22
colony, 11

D
dams, 21

E
Eurasian beavers, 7
Europe, 7

F
fur(s), 4, 8, 22

K
kit(s), 17–18

L
litters, 7, 17
lodge(s), 11, 18, 21

M
mammals, 4
Mexico, 7

O
oil glands, 8

P
pollutants, 21

S
scales, 14

T
tail(s), 4, 7–8, 14
trees, 4, 11

U
United States, 7

W
wetlands, 21
wood, 4, 11

Web Sites

Due to the changing nature of Internet links, PowerKids Press has developed an online list of Web sites related to the subject of this book. This site is updated regularly. Please use this link to access the list:
www.powerkidslinks.com/scat/beaver/

ML   3/09